Storytime Stickers

SHARKS AT SEA

Carol Murray

Illustrated by
Gary LaCoste

STERLING and the distinctive Sterling logo are
registered trademarks of Sterling Publishing Co., Inc.

Lot#:
6 8 10 9 7 5
08/10

Published by Sterling Publishing Co., Inc.
387 Park Avenue South, New York, NY 10016
Text © 2008 by Sterling Publishing Co., Inc.
Illustrations © 2008 by Gary LaCoste
Distributed in Canada by Sterling Publishing
c/o Canadian Manda Group, 165 Dufferin Street
Toronto, Ontario, Canada M6K 3H6
Distributed in the United Kingdom by GMC Distribution Services
Castle Place, 166 High Street, Lewes, East Sussex, England BN7 1XU
Distributed in Australia by Capricorn Link (Australia) Pty. Ltd.
P.O. Box 704, Windsor, NSW 2756, Australia

Printed in China

Sterling ISBN 978-1-4027-4660-4

For information about custom editions, special sales, premium and
corporate purchases, please contact Sterling Special Sales
Department at 800-805-5489 or specialsales@sterlingpublishing.com.

STERLING

New York / London
www.sterlingpublishing.com/kids

Behold the shark! In canyons stark,
he dashes, darts, and flips.
Around about and in and out,
he splashes as he zips.

The young ones nag, "Let's play some tag.
We're bored as stones," they fuss.
"Let's have a race to Lighthouse Place.
You're it! You can't catch us!"

Through schools of fish, they swarm and swish,
upsetting snakes and snails.
They finally reach a sandy beach,
with shells, and whelks with tails.

Lost Island calls with rocky walls
and caverns to explore.
They catch some waves above the caves,
and surf—and surf some more.

And soon they find a different kind
of pleasure that will suit.
They ram and rip a treasure ship,
and eyeball all the lo t.

It would be cool to have a duel,
for those with saws and spikes.
At Crater Lake, they give and take,
with throws and thrusts and strikes.

A coral maze in evening's haze
will test their sonar power.
They take the reef, with great relief,
and nap—for just an hour.